GALILEO

GALILEO GALILEI

LEONARD EVERETT FISHER

MACMILLAN PUBLISHING COMPANY
New York

Maxwell Macmillan Canada   Toronto

Maxwell Macmillan International   New York   Oxford   Singapore   Sydney

CHRONOLOGY OF GALILEO (1564–1642)

1564 . . . . Born at Pisa, February 15

1574 . . . . Family moves to Florence

1575–78 . . . . Enrolled at school of Jesuit Monastery of Santa Maria di Vallombrosa

1581–85 . . . . Studies at the University of Pisa

1584 . . . . Discovers the law of the pendulum

1585 . . . . Experiments with floating objects

1589 . . . . Teaches mathematics at the University of Pisa

Experiments with principle of motion and falling objects

1592 . . . . Appointed professor of mathematics at the University of Padua

Constructs the first thermoscope to measure heat

1602 . . . . Experiments with magnetism

1609 . . . . Constructs a telescope

Is the first to see the moon close up

1610 . . . . Observes Jupiter's moons and Saturn's rings

Publishes *The Starry Messenger*

Leaves Padua and goes to Florence

Named mathematician-philosopher to Cosimo II de Medici, duke of Tuscany

Constructs and uses the first microscope

1613 . . . . Observes sunspots

Publishes *Letters on Sunspots*

1614–31 . . . . Warned by the Church to give up the idea that the sun is the center of the universe

1632 . . . . Publishes *Dialogue on the Two Great Systems of the World*

Is ordered to Rome to appear before the Inquisition

1633 . . . . Forced to retract findings

Confined to house in Arcetri

1637 . . . . Goes blind

1638 . . . . Publishes *Discourses and Mathematical Demonstrations Concerning Two New Sciences*

1642 . . . . Dies and is buried in Florence

With appreciation to Dr. David J. Helfand, Professor of Astrophysics, Columbia University

10 9 8 7 6 5 4 3 2 1

The text of this book is set in 13 pt. Meridien. The black-and-white paintings were rendered in acrylic paints on paper.

Library of Congress Cataloging-in-Publication Data
Fisher, Leonard Everett. Galileo / Leonard Everett Fisher. — 1st ed.   p.   cm. Summary: Examines the life and discoveries of the noted mathematician, physicist, and astronomer, whose work changed the course of science. ISBN 0-02-735235-8 1. Galilei, Galileo, 1564–1642—Biography—Juvenile literature. 2. Galilei, Galileo, 1564–1642—Pictorial works—Juvenile literature. 3. Astronomers—Italy—Biography—Juvenile literature. [1. Galileo, 1564–1642. 2. Scientists.] I. Title.
QB36.G2F57 1992   520'.92—dc20   [B]   91-31146

To Samuel Benjamin,
my grandson

Alle stelle con amore

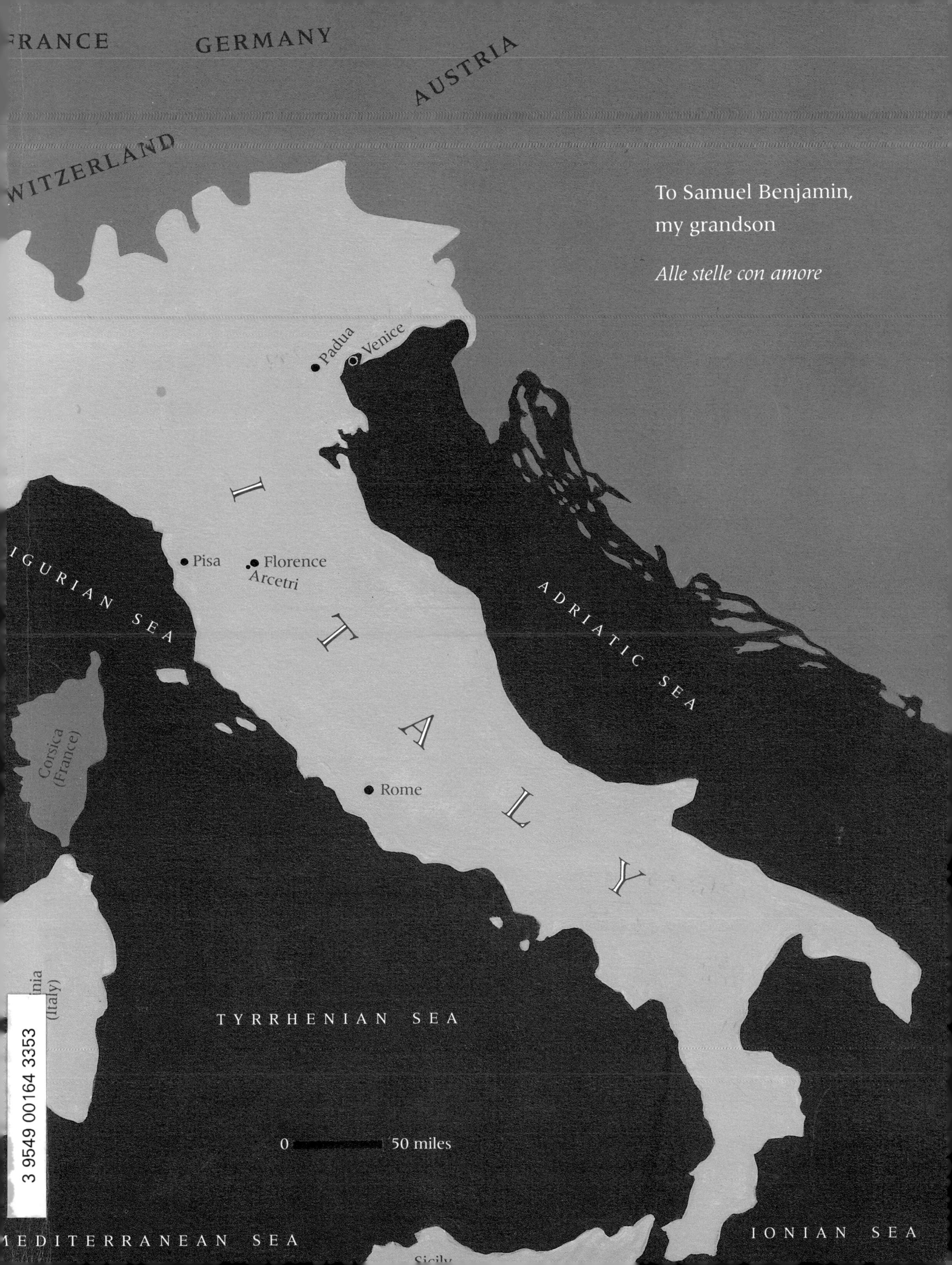

ITALY

Padua •   ○ Venice

LIGURIAN SEA

• Pisa   •• Florence
        Arcetri

ADRIATIC SEA

Corsica
(France)

• Rome

ITALY

TYRRHENIAN SEA

0   50 miles

MEDITERRANEAN SEA

IONIAN SEA

Sicily

I. Stellarum Fixarum Sphæra immobilis

II. Saturnus anno. XXX. revoluitur

III. Iouis. XII annorum revolutio

IIII. Martis bina revolutio

V. Telluris "
cum orbis lunari Annua revolutio
Terra

VI. Venus nonum dies
VII. Mercuri. rosse. Viginti

SoL

NICOLAUS COPERNICUS

The ancient Greek philosopher Aristotle believed that the earth was the center of the universe, standing still as the sun and stars traveled around it. And for centuries, the Roman Catholic Church considered this true.

In 1543 Nicolaus Copernicus, a Polish astronomer, wrote a book claiming that the sun was the center of the universe and that all heavenly bodies, including the earth, revolved around it. If his idea was correct, then the Church was wrong. Unfortunately, many Catholic clergymen did not believe that the Church could be mistaken.

Copernicus died that same year, 1543. It took a long time for his theory to become widely known. By 1616, the Copernican theory of the universe presented a major challenge to Church beliefs about the universe. The Church denounced it.

Galileo Galilei, a brilliant, lively, quick-tempered Italian mathematician, physicist, and astronomer—and a devout Catholic—set out to prove Copernicus right.

When Galileo was born in Pisa in 1564, a movement called the Reformation was sweeping across Catholic northern Germany. It had begun in 1517 as a protest by Martin Luther, a German priest concerned about the Church practice of selling papal indulgences—the privilege of not being punished for certain sins. France also seethed with religious disturbances. The Netherlands, England, and Scandinavia already had broken away from the authority of the Church. By 1564 a weakened Catholic Church was straining to check the continuing threat to its power and influence.

During this time of unrest, the Galilei family moved from Pisa to Florence, a center of learning and art. In 1575 eleven-year-old Galileo was sent to the school of the Jesuit Monastery of Santa Maria di Vallombrosa to study Latin, Greek, mathematics, religion, music, and painting.

At seventeen Galileo enrolled as a medical student at the University of Pisa. His financially strained family wanted him to become a rich doctor.

Three years later, while he was in the cathedral of Pisa, Galileo's attention was caught by a lamp swinging overhead. He timed its movements with the beat of his pulse. He discovered that each swing of the lamp, no matter how great or small, was equal in time. Twenty-year-old Galileo had recognized a simple truth—the law of the pendulum. The observation brought Galileo instant fame in the academic world.

In 1657 Galileo's discovery led the Dutch mathematician, physicist, and astronomer Christian Huygens to apply a pendulum in regulating a clock. The pendulum was then used to regulate most clocks for about two hundred and fifty years. Although some clocks, like grandfather clocks, are still regulated by a pendulum, today almost all clocks are regulated by electricity, which was introduced in the 1850s.

Galileo gave up the study of medicine. He was more interested in matter, energy, motion, and force—the science of physics. But after four years he had to leave the university without graduating. His family had become too poor to continue his education. Although scholarships were available, he was not offered one. The bright Galileo had grown unpopular for stubbornly demanding from his professors verification of the ancient beliefs that the sun traveled around the earth and that objects of different weights fell at different speeds. The professors would only reply that the Bible and the ancients were always right.

Over the next several years, Galileo mastered mathematics and physics with the help of a family friend, Ostilio Ricci, a professor of mathematics. During this period he experimented with floating objects. He developed the hydrostatic balance, a tool to measure accurately the specific gravity of a piece of some material: the weight of the piece when compared to an equal-sized volume of water. Galileo found that gold, for example, had a specific gravity of 19.3— which meant that any given piece of gold was always 19.3 times heavier than the same volume of water. Silver would always be 10.5 times heavier than the same volume of water. The measurement helped to identify substances like gold, silver, copper, and tin.

Galileo's reputation grew. In 1589, twenty-five-year-old Galileo, who had not been able to graduate from the University of Pisa, returned there as a professor of mathematics. He quickly made enemies by challenging a nearly two-thousand-year-old theory of Aristotle's.

It was Aristotle who had claimed that heavy objects fell to the earth faster than lighter ones. Galileo decided to prove that Aristotle was wrong. He dropped two balls of different weights at the same time from the same height at the top of a building, possibly the Leaning Tower of Pisa. A crowd of students and professors watched the balls land together. Those who were loyal followers of Aristotle refused to believe what they saw. They forced Galileo out of the university.

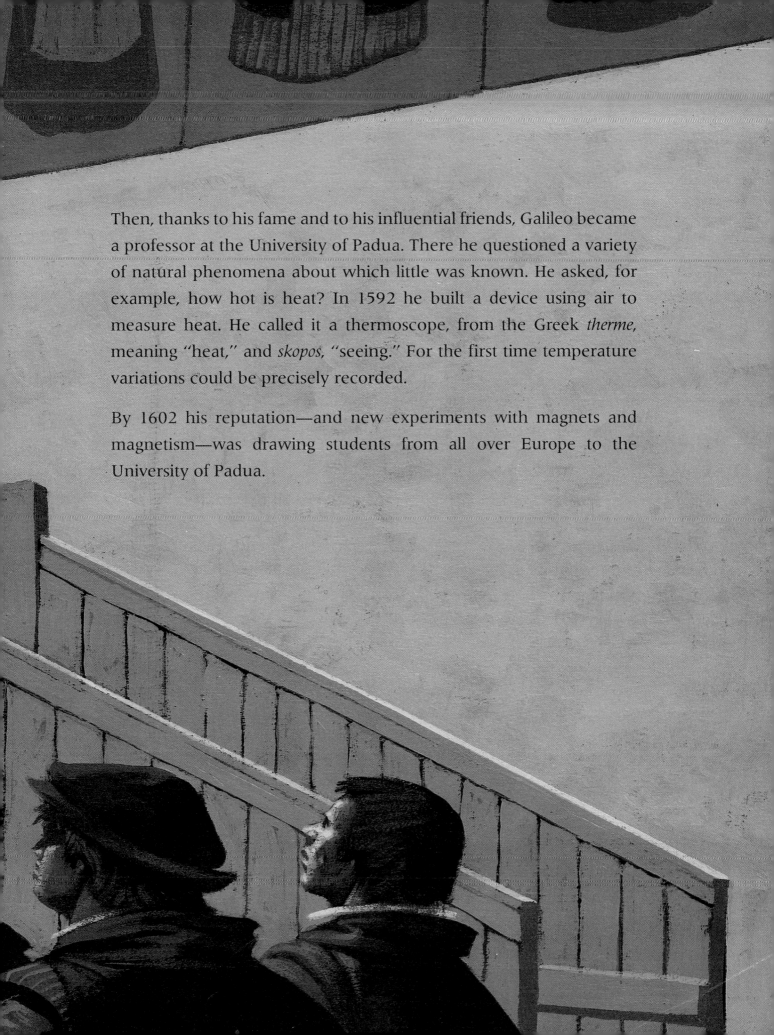

Then, thanks to his fame and to his influential friends, Galileo became a professor at the University of Padua. There he questioned a variety of natural phenomena about which little was known. He asked, for example, how hot is heat? In 1592 he built a device using air to measure heat. He called it a thermoscope, from the Greek *therme*, meaning "heat," and *skopos*, "seeing." For the first time temperature variations could be precisely recorded.

By 1602 his reputation—and new experiments with magnets and magnetism—was drawing students from all over Europe to the University of Padua.

right—that the moon was smooth and that Galileo was tricking himself
and everyone else.

In 1610 Galileo trained his spyglass on distant Jupiter. One night he saw near the planet four bright objects that no one had ever seen before. The next evening, he observed that they had changed positions. He realized they were Jupiter's own moons, traveling around the planet. Galileo began to think there was some truth to the Copernican idea that the earth was not the center of the universe.

Galileo published a small book, *The Starry Messenger*, in which he described what he saw. It was translated into a number of languages, and extended Galileo's fame around the world.

Galileo then began to make and sell his spyglasses all over Europe. Many people became as excited as he when they looked through the spyglass. But there were more who refused to use the spyglass and clung to the old beliefs.

In that same year, 1610, Galileo left Padua for Florence to become mathematician-philosopher to Cosimo II de Medici, the grand duke of Tuscany. It was a high position with a large salary. Now he could devote his entire attention to his investigations of nature.

To amuse his friends, Galileo built a magnifier for looking at insects. He called it a microscope, from the Greek *micros*, meaning "small," and *skopos*, "seeing."

By the year's end, Galileo had discovered what he thought were two stars circling Saturn. Christian Huygens later identified the "stars" as Saturn's rings.

Most important, Galileo watched the sunlight on Venus move across the planet just as the light does on our moon. And its phases—or changes from a full circle of light to a sliver of light—proved that Venus traveled around the sun, not the earth. Copernicus was right! The sun stood still as the planets and other heavenly bodies traveled around it. The earth was just another planet that, with its satellite, the moon, traveled around the sun.

Galileo went to Rome in 1611 to demonstrate his spyglass to Pope Paul V. The meeting was arranged by Maffeo Cardinal Barberini, a mathematician. Although the pope remained unimpressed, Galileo had some success. Prince Federico Cesi, a well-connected friend of Galileo's, gave banquets in his honor. At one dinner the prince and a poet, Johannes Demisiani, said that Galileo's spyglass deserved a better name. They combined the Greek words *tele*, or "far off," and *skopos*, meaning "seeing," and called it a *telescope*.

Galileo returned to Florence and discovered dark patches on the surface of the sun. In 1613 he published a paper on his finding, *Letters on Sunspots*. Pope Paul objected to the paper and to all of Galileo's heavenly explorations. He said these were dangerous to the faith, probably because they uncovered truths about which the Church knew nothing. Three years later, in 1616, the pope officially denounced the Copernican theory. Galileo was stunned.

In 1626 a group of powerful churchmen, professors, and local princes who had become enraged by Galileo's fame and growing fortune met to plot his ruin. The group included the once friendly Cardinal Barberini, who had become Pope Urban VIII on the death of Gregory XV in 1623 (Gregory had reigned for two years following the death of Pope Paul V). Urban thought that faith in Church doctrine was more important than the truth about nature. He urged Galileo to give up his belief that the sun was the center of the universe. The others told Galileo that since there was no account of his findings in the Bible, they were an illusion. Galileo promised to speak of the idea as a theory—only a possibility.

URBAN VIII

In 1632 Galileo could no longer deny what he knew was the truth. He published his *Dialogue on the Two Great Systems of the World* (the Church and science), in which three characters, one of whom was a yokel who seemed to be the pope, debated over whether the center of the universe was the sun or the earth. The book was a best-seller. Since it argued that the Church was wrong and appeared to be personally insulting, Pope Urban VIII banned the book.

The pope then ordered the sixty-eight-year-old, ailing Galileo to Rome to appear before the Holy Office of the Inquisition. Galileo was accused of upholding the Copernican theory of the universe after being warned not to. His crime was thought worse than the offenses of Martin Luther.

At first Galileo would not tell the judges of the Inquisition that he was wrong. However, he was too sick and exhausted to resist for long. His strongest supporter, Prince Cesi, had died. Another supporter, Cardinal Piccolomini, the Archbishop of Siena, was ignored. In 1633, after being confronted by fake documents and threatened with torture, he dressed himself in the white cloak of a sorrowful sinner and, on his knees, announced that Copernicus was wrong about the universe and that he, Galileo, was wrong to have publicly promoted such an idea.

He signed a paper attesting to his errors and was confined to his house in Arcetri, outside of Florence, for the rest of his life. At least he could be near his daughter, Virginia, a nun at an Arcetri convent. Galileo had two daughters—Virginia and Livia (who had died earlier)—and a son, Vincenzo, by Marina Gamba, whom he had never married. When Virginia died a year later, Galileo was crushed.

Despite his sadness, Galileo continued to ponder the universe at Arcetri. He was prohibited from writing or speaking about the Copernican theory of the universe, but nothing prevented him from expounding on the laws of force and motion.

In 1637, four years after being imprisoned in his house, Galileo became totally blinded by an infection. His son and two former students came to help him and remained as valuable assistants.

The following year, 1638, he published his *Discourses and Mathematical Demonstrations Concerning Two New Sciences* (force and motion). The book made it possible for Sir Isaac Newton, an English mathematician, to discover the laws of gravity and motion twenty-seven years later.

Galileo Galilei is rightly called the father of modern science. Through his experiments, to which he applied the laws of mathematics and logic, he showed the importance of testing ideas.

When Galileo died in 1642, he was still considered guilty of spreading beliefs that were contrary to Church teachings. Pope Urban VIII, who outlived him by two years, never forgave Galileo for his disobedience. Urban was so angry that he refused to allow a statue of Galileo to be erected in front of the Church of Santa Croce in Florence, where Galileo was buried.

Galileo remained guilty in the eyes of the Church for more than three hundred years, even though the ban on his *Dialogue* was removed in 1822. By then the whole world knew that the earth traveled around the sun.

During the second Vatican Council, 1962–65, the Church addressed the issue of Galileo's guilt and appeared to pardon him when it stated that "if methodical investigation…is carried out in a genuinely scientific manner…it never truly conflicts with faith." It was not until 1979, however, that Pope John Paul II clearly acknowledged the truth of Galileo's arguments and those of Copernicus. "Galileo…suffered at the hands of…the Church," the pope declared.

By July 1984, the Pontifical Academy of Sciences in Rome had taken steps to clear Galileo. The Church finally seemed to believe what Césare Cardinal Baronio had said in 1615, the year before Copernicus's theory was denounced: "The Bible tells us how to make it to Heaven, not how Heaven is made."